WALT DISNEY'S

Peter Pan

Late one night, high above London, a figure dressed in green soared across the starry sky. It was Peter Pan! Along with him flew his trusted friend, a pixie named Tinker Bell.

Peter and Tinker Bell landed outside the Darling family's nursery window. Inside, Wendy, John, and Michael Darling were fast asleep. Peter sneaked in without a sound and began to look for his shadow. He had left it behind the last time he had come to visit the nursery—and he needed it back.

Soon, Peter found his shadow, but not before he had accidentally knocked over a small table. The noise woke up Wendy—and soon Michael and John were up, too.

Peter convinced the children to come back with him to Never Land. "But, Peter, how do we get there?" Wendy asked.

"Fly, of course!" Peter answered.

And with that, Tinker Bell sprinkled pixie dust over them. In no time at all, the children were flying through the nursery window and out into the night sky. Peter Pan led the way, heading toward the second star to the right and straight on until morning. At last, they looked down and saw a beautiful island.

"Oh, look! There's Cap'n Hook and the pirates!" cried Michael, pointing down below. Sure enough, Michael had spotted Captain Hook's ship.

But Captain Hook had also spotted them. He wanted nothing more than to blast that annoying Peter Pan right out of the sky. So he ordered his men to shoot a cannonball straight at Peter and the children.

Whizzz! Luckily, the cannonball missed them. But Captain Hook was not finished yet! The pirates fired another shot.

Peter Pan stayed behind to draw Hook's fire while Tinker Bell led the children down to the island.

The little fairy was flying so quickly, the children could not keep up. In fact, Tinker Bell was trying to leave them behind. She was very jealous of Wendy. So she raced ahead to Peter's hideout. There, she told the Lost Boys that Peter Pan wanted them to shoot at Wendy.

The Lost Boys took aim with their slingshots, and soon a shower of stones flew toward Wendy. She lost control and began to fall out of the sky!

Just then, Peter Pan swooped down from out of nowhere and caught her. "Oh, Peter, you saved my life!" she cried.

When everyone was safely on the ground, Peter Pan introduced the children to the Lost Boys. Then, as Michael, John, and the Lost Boys went off to explore the island, Peter Pan took Wendy to Mermaid Lagoon.

Soon, Peter heard a sound. It was a faint ticktocking—it sounded just like the crocodile that was always following Captain Hook!

Peter and Wendy flew off toward the sound and trailed Captain Hook to Skull Rock. He was with his first mate, Smee. They had kidnapped the Indian princess, Tiger Lily.

"You tell me the hiding place of Peter Pan," Captain Hook said to Tiger Lily, "and I shall set you free."

But Tiger Lily refused to reveal the secret. So, Hook left her tied up in the watery cave. When the tide came in, Tiger Lily would drown! It was up to Peter Pan to rescue her!

Before long, Peter Pan and Captain Hook were locked in a duel. Peter thought it was great fun. He flew all around him and landed on Hook's blade.

Finally, Peter Pan lured the pirate off a rocky ledge. At the last minute, Captain Hook managed to grab the ledge with his hook. But suddenly, the rock gave way, and he splashed down into the water.

Smee rushed to save Captain Hook. As the captain climbed into the rowboat, the hungry crocodile chased the two of them away.

Meanwhile, Peter Pan rescued Tiger Lily in the nick of time and flew her back to the Indian camp. The Indian chief was so grateful, he gave Peter the name "Chief Little Flying Eagle."

When it was time to go back home, Peter sailed Wendy and her brothers back to London on a magical pirate ship.

It was only the first of many adventures that they would have with Peter Pan.